W9-CZW-570

# LeBron James

## YOUNG BASKETBALL STAR

by
Joanne Mattern

P.O. Box 196
Hockessin, Delaware 19707
Visit us on the web: www.mitchelllane.com
Comments? email us: mitchelllane@mitchelllane.com

Printing            2          3          4          5          6          7          8

**A Robbie Reader**

| | | |
|---|---|---|
| Hillary Duff | Thomas Edison | Albert Einstein |
| Philo T. Farnsworth | Henry Ford | Robert Goddard |
| Mia Hamm | Tony Hawk | **LeBron James** |
| Donovan McNabb | Dr. Seuss | Charles Schulz |

Library of Congress Cataloging-in-Publication Data
Mattern, Joanne, 1963-
    LeBron James/ by Joanne Mattern.
       p. cm. — (A Robbie reader)
    Includes bibliographical references and index.
    ISBN 1-58415-293-1 (library bound)
    1. James, LeBron—Juvenile literature.  2. Basketball players—United States—Biography—Juvenile literature.  I. Title. II. Series.
    GV884.J36M38 2005
    796.323′092—dc22
                                            2004009304

**ABOUT THE AUTHOR:** Joanne Mattern is the author of more than 100 nonfiction books for children. Along with biographies, she has written extensively about animals, nature, history, sports, and foreign cultures. She lives near New York City with her husband and two young daughters.

**PHOTO CREDITS:** Cover: Getty Images; p. 4 Matt Campbell/EPA Photo; p. 6 Johnny Nunez/WireImage; p. 8 Andrea Renault/Globe Photos, Inc.; p. 10 Steve Grayson/WireImage; p. 12 Dave Saffran/WireImage; p. 14 Johnny Nunez/WireImage; p. 16 Steve Grayson/WireImage; p. 18 Lisa Blumenfeld/Getty Images; p. 20 Tom Pidgeon/Getty Images; p. 21 Linda Spillers/WireImage; p. 22 Ron Schwane/AP Photo;  pp. 24, 25 Steve Grayson/WireImage; p. 26 Steven Dunn/Getty Images; p. 27 Johnny Nunez/WireImage; p. 28 Newsday.

**ACKNOWLEDGMENTS:**  The following story has been thoroughly researched, and to the best of our knowledge, represents a true story. While every possible effort has been made to ensure accuracy, the publisher will not assume liability for damages caused by inaccuracies in the data, and makes no warranty on the accuracy of the information contained herein. This story has not been authorized nor endorsed by LeBron James.

# TABLE OF CONTENTS

LeBron with NBA Commissioner David Stern soon after the Cleveland Cavaliers picked LeBron as their first choice in the 2003 NBA draft.

# FIRST PICK

The crowd in Madison Square Garden in New York City buzzed with excitement. They were waiting to hear who would be the first pick in the 2003 NBA (National Basketball Association) draft. A draft is when different teams pick new players.

A man named David Stern stepped up to the microphone. He was the **commissioner** of the NBA. Stern said, "With the first pick of the 2003 NBA draft, the Cleveland Cavaliers select LeBron James."

LeBron was happy to be picked by the Cleveland Cavaliers. Here he is celebrating with his mother and a friend after the NBA draft.

Everyone cheered. No one was surprised that the Cavaliers picked LeBron. People had been talking about LeBron for years. He was a very good player. People were excited that he would finally play in the NBA.

There was one more thing that made LeBron James special. He was only 18 years old. He had just graduated from high school. LeBron would be one of the few high school players to go right to an NBA team.

After the draft, LeBron talked to news reporters. He said, "I just have to go out there and play hard and play strong and help my teammates every night." LeBron knew all about playing hard and helping his team. Basketball had been the center of his life since he was a child.

By 2003, LeBron had come a long way from his difficult childhood. He was such a big star that he was invited to the MTV Music Awards.

# LIFE ON HICKORY STREET

LeBron James was born on December 30, 1984. He was born in Akron, Ohio. LeBron's mother was Gloria James. Gloria was only 16 years old when her son was born. LeBron's father was not a part of his life.

Gloria worked hard to support herself and her baby. The little family moved from one apartment to another. They were always looking for a better way to live.

When LeBron was eight months old, his mother met a man named Eddie Jackson. Eddie became part of the James family. LeBron calls Eddie his father.

After a poor childhood, LeBron enjoyed the fame and riches of playing professional basketball.

Gloria, Eddie, and LeBron moved in with Gloria's mother, Freda. The family lived in a little house on Hickory Street in Akron. The people on Hickory Street did not have a lot of money, but they kept their houses looking nice. It was a friendly neighborhood.

When LeBron was little, he liked rough games. Eddie Jackson used to wrestle with LeBron. The little boy liked to jump off the couch on top of his father.

When LeBron was three years old, Gloria and Eddie bought him a special Christmas present. It was a basketball set. They set up the set on Christmas Eve. When the little boy woke on Christmas morning, he was so excited! LeBron loved his new toy.

That Christmas was a happy time for LeBron. But it was a sad day for Gloria and Eddie. Early that morning, Freda James died of a heart attack. Gloria did not tell LeBron what happened until later. She wanted him to enjoy his Christmas.

Sports were a big part of LeBron's childhood. He competed in many high school tournaments, including the Trenton High School Shootout where he is shown in this photo.

# SAVED BY SPORTS

After Freda died, Gloria had to move away from Hickory Street. Gloria and LeBron moved from one bad neighborhood to another. There was a lot of **violence** in these places. LeBron stayed close to his mother and kept out of trouble.

Sometimes Gloria got in trouble with the police. Gloria's troubles hurt LeBron. They made it hard for him in school. In fourth grade, he missed more than half the school year.

LeBron lived with his coach, Frankie Walker, Sr., for part of his childhood. He became an important part of the Walker family. Here, LeBron poses with Walker's son, Frankie, Jr.

LeBron was friends with a local coach named Frankie Walker. The Walkers invited LeBron to live with them. LeBron became part of their family. He had to follow the rules and go to school. LeBron lived with the Walkers during the week. On weekends, he stayed with his mother.

When LeBron was 10 years old, Frankie Walker taught him how to play basketball. LeBron learned fast. Soon he was on Walker's team. LeBron also worked with younger players as an **assistant** coach.

When he was in eighth grade, LeBron was one of the best players in Akron. Basketball would soon change his life forever.

LeBron loved the excitement of playing basketball for Saint Vincent-Saint Mary, a private high school in Akron.

# HIGH SCHOOL STAR

St. Vincent–St. Mary was a private school in Akron. The school wanted LeBron to play basketball for them. They gave LeBron a **scholarship** to go to the school and be on the basketball team. LeBron was happy to accept.

LeBron soon became a star at St. Vincent–St. Mary (SVSM). When he was in 10th grade, he was called one of the best basketball players in the country. LeBron helped SVSM win three state championships.

LeBron played football too. He was a big, strong teenager. He was six feet, eight inches tall. He weighed about 245 pounds.

LeBron worked and played hard as a member of the Saint Vincent-Saint Mary team.

People all over the country heard about LeBron. He won many awards. **Scouts** from **professional** basketball teams came to see LeBron play. They liked the way LeBron could shoot, pass, and score. The scouts also liked that LeBron was a team player.

LeBron wanted to play in the NBA. But the NBA had a rule that said a player had to finish high school before he could play in the league. When LeBron was in 11th grade, he wanted to change that rule. He told reporters that he wanted to be in the NBA draft that year.

LeBron was a star on the court, but he was also a strong team player who helped his high-school teammates score.

LeBron thought long and hard about whether he should stay in high school. He talked to his mother. He talked to his coach. Finally, LeBron announced that he would finish high school. He wanted to play with his friends and be part of their team.

LeBron had a great senior year. In June, he graduated from SVSM with good grades. His high school days were over. Now it was time to join the NBA.

In 2003, LeBron played in the Jordan Capital Classic. He shared the Most Valuable Player Award with Shannon Brown (right).

LeBron dunks the ball against the Denver Nuggets on November 5, 2003 in Cleveland, Ohio.

# LEBRON MAKES IT BIG

In 2003, the Cleveland Cavaliers had the number one pick for the 2003 draft. It was no surprise when they picked LeBron as their first choice.

Many new players have trouble in the NBA because they don't have a lot of **experience** playing professional basketball. Most people felt that LeBron would do well. He was a great player. He believed in himself. Most of all, he was a team player who worked well with others.

LeBron signed a contract to promote Nike's clothes and shoes. Here he is shooting a commercial for Nike.

LeBron had a very successful first season with the Cavaliers. He played guard and scored 25 points in his first NBA game. He **averaged** about 20 points a game for the season. During one game in February 2004, he scored 38 points. In April 2004, LeBron was named NBA **Rookie** of the Year.

Basketball made LeBron a rich man. Before he joined the NBA, Nike (NYE-kee) gave him a deal worth $90 million to wear Nike sneakers and clothes. Life was very different than it was when he grew up in a poor family in rough neighborhoods.

LeBron watches himself on TV in the Nike sneaker commercial.

Gloria James is proud to let everyone know she is "LeBron's Mom."

So far, LeBron has done a fine job handling his fame and wealth. He is very close to his mother. LeBron says Gloria is everything to him. Gloria goes to almost all of his games. She proudly wears a shirt that says "LeBron's Mom" on it.

"Basketball has made my life fun," LeBron once said. Millions of people have had fun watching him make his mark on basketball and life.

After LeBron won the NBA Rookie of the Year award, he posed with Julius Irving (right), a basketball star from the 1970s.

LeBron plays hard in every game. He is one of the best rookie basketball players.

1984    LeBron James is born in Akron, Ohio, on December 30.

1994    LeBron moves in with his coach, Frankie Walker, and begins playing basketball.

1999    LeBron begins attending St. Vincent–St. Mary High School on a basketball scholarship.

2001– 2003   LeBron leads his high school team to three state championships.

2003    LeBron signs a $90 million deal with Nike.

On June 26, he is selected by the Cleveland Cavaliers as the first pick in the NBA draft.

On October 7, LeBron plays in his first professional basketball game.

2004    LeBron is named NBA Rookie of the Year.

"LeBron James." Biography Resource Center Online. Gale Group, 2003. http://galenet.galegroup.com/servlet/BioRC

Morgan, David Lee, Jr. "LeBron's Journey." *Sports Illustrated for Kids,* January 2004, volume 16, issue 1, page 27.

Rhodes, Joe. "The Golden Cav." *TV Guide,* February 21–27, 2004, page 51.

Wahl, Grant. "Ahead of His Class." *Sports Illustrated,* February 18, 2002, volume 96, issue 7, page 62.

Web Addresses

Cleveland.com
http://cleveland.com/lebron

ESPN.com: LeBron James
http://www.sports.espn.com/nba/players/profile?statsid=3704

LeBron James
http://www.lebronjames.com

**assistant** (uh-SIS-tent)—a person who helps someone do a job

**averaged** (AV-ridj'd)—to get an average number, which is the number found by adding a group of figures together and then dividing the sum by the number of figures; to get about the same number of something, such as points, every time.

**commissioner** (kuh-MISH-uh-nuhr)—the leader of an organization

**experience** (ex-PEER-ee-ents)—knowledge and skills gained by doing something

**professional** (pruh-FEH-shuh-nuhl)—someone who is paid for a job

rookie (RUH-kee)—an athlete in his or her first season with the team

**scholarship** (SKAH-luhr-ship)—money given to someone to pay for school

**scouts** (SKOWTS)—people who go out to study something and then bring back information about it

**violence** (VY-uh-lents)—the use of physical force to injure someone or damage something